MW01505670

Penmanship Books
Published by Penmanship Publishing Group
593 Vanderbilt Avenue, #265
Bklyn, NY 11238

First Penmanship trade edition: September 2006

To contact Jaha Zainabu please visit
www.myspace.com/jahazainabu
www.penmanshipbooks.com

Printed in The United States of America

10 9 8 7 6 5 4 3 2 1

This book is dedicated to fish.
This book is dedicated to friends.
This book is dedicated to my freedom.
This book is dedicated to love.
This book is dedicated to my destination.
This book is dedicated to the color red.
This book is dedicated to inspiration.
This book is dedicated to my imagination.
This book is dedicated to the trees in my backyard.
This book is dedicated to the sun.
This book is dedicated to the deer next to my fence.
This book is dedicated to my journey.
This book is dedicated to my life.
This book is dedicated to my spirit.
This book is dedicated to doing it the way I do it.
This book is dedicated to family.
This book is dedicated to McDonough.
This book is dedicated to Los Angeles.
This book is dedicated to Long Beach.
This book is dedicated to grandmothers.
This book is dedicated to my vagina.
This book is dedicated to my breasts.
This book is dedicated to laughing.
This book is dedicated to music.
This book is dedicated to Africa.
This book is dedicated to black people.
This book is dedicated to white people.
This book is dedicated to women.
This book is dedicated to men.
This book is dedicated to relationships.
This book is dedicated to sex.
This book is dedicated to myspace.
This book is dedicated to hotmail.
This book is dedicated to Georgia.
This book is dedicated to California.
This book is dedicated to poetry.

This book is dedicated to stories.
This book is dedicated to books.
This book is dedicated to children.
This book is dedicated to mothers. Did I already say mothers?
This book is dedicated to merlot.
This book is dedicated to work.
This book is dedicated to passion.
This book is dedicated to the moon.
This book is dedicated to traffic?
This book is dedicated to watermelon.

Special Thanks to:

The one Most High God who is the Source of all of my Supply.
Uraeus Orion Allison. My son / lesson / blessing. Thank you.
My mother Patricia Turner. I love you dearly. Thank you will
never be big enough.
Imani Tolliver, my partner in prayer.
My sister Roshann.
My brother George
V Kali, because you exist and I get to know you. I get to love you.
Laura Colbert, for listening, for knowing, for loving, for sharing.
Bridget Gray, for being a friend.
Brad and Joan Sanders, for holding us in prayer

This book is dedicated to Robin Reed.
STORY STORY STORY
DRAMA DRAMA DRAMA
LIVE YOUR LIFE AND
GET OVER IT
OKAY?
OKAY.

THE CORNERS OF MY SHAPING
Contents
Poems
Stories
Musings
Prayers
Stuff
Stream of consciousness

**Just open it and read it.
Ok?**

Also by Jaha Zainabu

THE SCIENCE OF CHOCOLATE MILK MAKING poetry, musings, stories
THE NIKEL novella
THE JUNGLE STORY short story
JOURNEY CD 2001
UNMASKED CD 2003

THE CORNERS OF MY SHAPING
Introduction

Every writer sets out to write the book that will change the
world. Change the world? At
this point in my life I just wanna let it out. Finally. Honestly. My
own stories. My own
life. Breathe in and out with no lingering stories there nagging to
get out. And right now,
they are nagging. Memories, stories, self-conversations popping
up at unsuitable times.
But are the times ever...unsuitable? They come, I feel, when they
are ready to be handled
with care, written about, sketched out, set free.
Life is what it is. We are dealt the cards we're dealt and
expectantly play the best hand
we can play. I have humbly learned that I am not the accretion of
my stories. I am not my
bank statements or career choices, height or marital status. Not
my gender or shoe size or
gynecological appointments, kept or no. I am not any of the
definitions I have used to
describe myself. Woman, lover, mother, daughter, writer, sister,
friend, artist, dot, dot,
dot. I am infinite possibilities and have decided to embrace all of
who I am, and who I am
not. I embrace all of my experiences, understanding that I needed
them to form me into
who I am today. *Wouldn't take nothing for my journey now.* My
experiences are, each of
them, the pleasant ones and those that still hurt too much to
mention, plainly the corners
of my shaping.
I, right now, abdicate my position of right and faultless knowing
that it never existed,

accepting that it doesn't matter anyway. I also release, right here in these pages, my
stories. Ok, some of them. I am now of the understanding that what has happened in my
life and my stories about what has happened in my life are separate. The drama has
always come with me trying to make them the same. They are not. What happened is
what happened. I created my stories from my own background and sensitivities and ran
with it. Called enough people to validate my point of view and there you have it. Me, the
self appointed victim of my life, choosing to pay more attention to the ebb than the flow.
I accept that as I created that position, I am powerful enough to create a new reality. I
heretofore create a space and possibility of a life of me achieving my goals, loving myself
fully and accepting others as I love and accept myself. I create right now a journey of
success and lessons learned and love given and received. And so it is.
Sometimes I wish I could break through the stars to the top of the moon in the middle of
the night and wake everybody up with my hands on my hips (lettin' my backbone slip)
and stompin' my feet and screamin' loud as I can "THIS IS ME, WORLD! THIS IS WHO
I AM. I think."

Scream

Sometimes it's in you
Just in you
Gotta come out
Don't matter none
That it don't make sense to nobody

Not even you
Especially you
It don't matter none
That you can't sing
Or write a poem
Tell no story
Nothin' like that
What difference it make
Don't nobody wanna hear it
Or if you aint got nobody to tell
No how

It's a funny thing, me revisiting journals. There is always this
urge to edit and pretend
that I was always this...wise...woman. (lol) I wasn't. Who was?
Am I even now? I am
honoring myself for the courage to read my journals from
forever ago and love the
young, silly girl. Sure I would love to retype them and when he
said...and called me a...I
looked at him square in the face and said...! Grabbed my bag and
walked out and
slammed the door! But I didn't. I cried. Hoped he would stay.

There is no place to begin to tell your story, only a place you choose to start. Because
later you find places to begin before that moment and you try to go back. And then it
happens again. There are places even before that. I am thankful for those places. Those
before and before places that allow me the reasons I need to justify my procrastination.
Too many reasons to hold on to stories. But they are lies. Every voice in my head that
tells me I am not good enough. Every whisper that shouts and threatens to tell the world
(what the world already knows) that I am a human being. Perfect in all of my
imperfections. Beautiful in my ugly.

It is in that space of uncertainty where we have best opportunity to co-create (with God) our lives. To be powerfully present. Letting go of what we already know. Creating an existence, a reality from nothing. From only the blessed space that God gave. The glorious abyss of infinite possibilities. In that space, there are only our dreams. We choose them small or big.

06-22-01 / 4:03 am / The Palm Motel
I'm going to go walking.

God is good. God is good. I am at peace with my life. I love myself.
I am happy with who I am. I am happy with who I am.

*Note here, the entries in your journals when you're reminding
yourself of how happy you were over and over. Sometimes you
weren't.

Prayer Haiku

Dear God I surren
Der to it all to Your will be
Cause you know better

The truck stalled today and I was really frustrated. While I was at the pay phone, this homeless woman tried to get into the truck. In that moment I wasn't so frustrated about the stalled truck. I was glad I had a home.

Just Things

When my son was in the first grade he was in a math competition in his class. Easy rules. Whoever answered the math questions correctly first was the winner. The winner of this fierce competition, that lasted twenty minutes (maybe), would get a package of flexipencils.
Twelve of them. I mean, FLEXI-PENCILS! TWELVE OF THEM!

When I picked him up from school that day he got into the car with a solemn look on his face. I knew that he did not win. I felt... sad? because he felt sad. I knew that he knew the answers to the math questions. All of them. I was also aware of what he made the prize mean. Him receiving flexi-pencils from the teacher that day in front of his peers would have meant (to him, and to his classmates) that he was smart, wonderful, special, a great person. The list goes on. Uraeus, my wonderful son, is already awesome, already incredible, already all of it. Flexi-pencils, by the way, are just pencils that bend. And not all the way mind you. But more than regular pencils do. A package of twelve I think are $1.29. The ones with SpongeBob's face on them are sixty cents more, I think. Anyway, flexi-pencils do not define Uraeus. I began to think about how often we chase things and people and prizes because someone gave them a special meaning and we dedicated our lives to achieving them without stopping to recognize that these prizes, all of them are flexi-pencils. Understand here that I am not saying that flexi-pencils are meaningless. Instead I am saying that they mean exactly what we make them mean. The prizes in our lives mean what we make them mean. The hardships we go through mean what we make them mean. We shape them with our words, our dreams. What we believe.

Play

My mama yo mama hangin' out some clothes
My mama socked yo mama in the nose
Did it hurt!?!
No!
Did it hurt!?!
No!
(from a girls jump rope song 'cause that's how we had fun)

In 1973 my sunny days began and ended with me sitting
impassively on my front steps. My castle. Not like many children
today who seem to require expensive electronic gadgets to
occupy themselves. I could caper around busying my inquisitive
mind for
hours on end on my steps counting perfectly the cars that went
by. Ford, Ford, Toyota, Pinto. Pretending I was the exquisite
Diahann Carroll giving an eloquent speech to my loyal fans, head
held high and tilted, looking down beyond my pointed nose, hair
curled
and poofey and perfect like a high fashioned helmet, or pressed
straight and pulled back tight in a bun. Me, being a queen on my
royal grounds where I first loved the smell of water tasting
thirsty sidewalk on hot days and California cold nights. Where
the smell of grass was my favorite fluffy lounge chair at
Starbucks and chamomile tea. Though I did not drink tea in those
days. And there was no Starbucks. Where there was my tree, just
nine papa steps in front of my porch. Whose leaves and branches
reached to God's house and hung almost to the grass but were
not strong enough to hold me. Yet assured me that I was strong
enough to brook whatever should come my way. That I was okay.
My front steps. I have blocked out, or it has been blocked out for
me, some of the details of this story, but that part is clear, those
were my steps. There were only three and that was perfect.
My mom, dad and I had recently moved from the green (or was it
brown?) apartment building on Walnut in Central Long Beach

commonly known as the east side, to the single family dwellings
on the west side of town at 1367 Cameron. Right around the
corner from both sets of my grandparents who lived on Taper
Street across from each other. In the apartment on Walnut,
before my sister Roshann was born, we lived on the
second floor. The steps were ugly and concrete and cobblestone.
There was a peek a boo space between each step and a black iron
rod to hold onto as one traversed up and down.

But those steps were not mine. No. They belonged to everyone.
And no one claimed them as their own. No one dreamed of
having long brown hair and marrying a prince on those steps.
Those steps were not my friends. I would not tell my secrets
there. One day I was in the living room and the door was left
open. I was finally, to the surprise of my parents, tall enough to
open the screen door. A screen that barely held out flies. An easy
unlock.

My tricycle was parked at the top of the steps and was blue and
had white strips of plastic hanging from the handlebars to flitter
in the wind as I rocketed by. I opened the door and I was on the
top of the steps. I sat there wondering, visualizing myself gliding
down on
my tricycle. I fancied my plastic strips waving away in the wind.
Like fire. A delightful way to spend an uneventful Sunday
afternoon. The coast was clear and I went for it. God is wonderful
in what He allows us to forget. I don't remember tumbling all the
way down, but I must have. About five years later I fell and was
in the intensive care unit at Memorial Hospital for two weeks
with a fractured skull from another fall. Again, I
remember falling, but not the hitting the ground part. God is
wonderful. From the stairs I do remember landing and crying at
the bottom step. I remember being hurt, but safe.
Mostly I suppose I was disappointed. That was not what I had
envisioned. There were three teenaged boys strolling by who
thought without thinking that my tumbling was funny. My father,

annoyed by their mocking and buffoonery and suddenly sobered
from
Schlitz Malt Liquor and Mary Jane, reminded them in his special
way, that surely it was not. My Cameron Street steps were not
disappointing like those. They did not call out to me with the
intent of temptation when I was momentarily unsupervised.
They did not propose excitement on a peaceful Sunday and then
produce danger. My new steps did not lie. I was only safe on
those steps that were red and three and my own.
Next door on Cameron, west of us, in the green house where I do
not recall a mommy or daddy (but there must have been at least
a mommy) lived two girls whose names and faces I can never call
to mind. I have not outgrown their voices however, raspy and
bumptious, heavy for such thin girls as it occurs to me in my
hindsight. They had cool sneakers and strong arms, cold fingers
and could Double Dutch a full song. Indeed they were real.
Though I have had lovers who wished they were not. I remember
them to be about fifteen and sixteen. My mother remembers that
too. The oldest lead the ghetto bureaucracy. In short, she was the
boss of us. Of her sister, who was taller with shorter
hair, quiet with issues of her own brewing with no place to
unfold. Of me, lucky and next door. Of what seemed like the
neighborhood where each house appeared occupied with private
business. After some time it was okay with my parents that I
went in their backyard with them that shared the same fence as
ours. Whose grass was the same green. That was the same size
and also had pomegranate and lemon trees and a garage and no
dog. We did not have a dog yet. But theirs was not mine. They
had a white tent behind the garage and a nephew who was a few
years older than I and shy. There was also a big boy, a teenager
or older in the tent. I do not remember his name. Almost his
voice. Barely
his hair that was short like big boys wore their hair. Faded blue
jeans slightly too big and looked clean but were not. Was callow
and slim but had burly black boy sad eyes that had been in

20

trouble before with full lips and a half happy smile poked and held to one side.

The oldest was the cagey heavy whisperer of the cabal. Something was up. I saw the fusee signals and heard the cacophony of voices in my head but crossed the line anyway.

I was four and they demanded I stop being a big baby and suck his dick. I remember that it had never been a dick before. Somehow I knew that boys had pee pees, but dicks were new. Perhaps pee pees grew into dicks, I must have thought. But my young Virgo analyzing and attention to the byplay was not going to postpone this. There was a dick in front of me and big girls I thought were my friends begging in their demanding voices to suck. But it was not peppermint or Bit o Honey, more like a Bomb Pop or Big Stick. But not from the ice cream truck with bells and whistles. It was not smooth and orange and sweet and inviting. It was Play-Do left open. Ashy and uncared for. I wanted my steps. This was my first dick and I wanted my steps that were safe and red and lead to my porch, where there was dust and loose gravel and chipped paint and no dicks. My porch had no dicks. But I was far away from my porch. Far from my lawn never perfectly manicured but mine. Just next door but miles from my father who would beat that dick up if he knew. Far from my mother who would spank their big girl butts if she knew that her daughter, who was sugar and spice and everything nice, was not sucking at all. Was gagging on flesh too big for her mouth, too hard for her jaws, too long for her throat. A dick. Even the name was not nice. If my father knew... If my mother knew... What if I was not everything nice anymore? I did not like her yelling hand with dark brown rough knuckles on the back of my head touching too firmly my barrettes that were red and friendly like my porch. Did not like the bossy one moaning like it felt good to her. Her eyes half closed and head moving passionately in half circle then back again. The slow inhale hiss and ahh. Like I was doing it right. Then from nowhere there was liquid that was warm and salty and not my spit

21

anymore. I ran out of the tent screaming. "He peed in my mouth! He peed in my mouth!" I ran as fast as I could to get past my porch, that was just a porch and not safe, into my bed, my for real castle. Before I could get to the gate the shorthaired one caught me. I kicked and screamed but she carried me to the t shaped clothesline post that was strong and sturdy. Like maybe this was for more than sun drying skirts and blouses to be worn on Sundays. Maybe for other girls who had pee in their mouths and ran to get away.

She tied thick brown rope around my neck and tied the other end to the top of the post. She picked me up and held my body as it swung. Surely that was a station for girls who did not swallow pee. For girls who could not run faster than a fifteen year old and threatened to tell. This was a four year olds Calvary. She told me that I would not say anything because if I did she would tell my mother that it was all my idea and I was a nasty girl. Me?
My mother could not believe that I was a nasty bad girl. But what if she did?
What if I was?
She let me go with a shove that said all I needed to know. I was too scared to tell my mother, too scared to tell my father. That night when it was time for bath my mother noticed the rope burn around my neck. I lied to her about how I got it. Told her that I was playing some game and it didn't even hurt. My mother, being a mother, wasn't satisfied with the story. I couldn't go in their backyard anymore. I couldn't be with the girls at all.

Fine with me.

I don't remember the speech after the bath. Don't remember what happened to the dick or the nephew. I vaguely recall the girls after that. I do remember that my steps were too close to theirs. They were not my steps anymore. There was a dick.

In the sixth grade Big Pam pushed me down and I was too afraid of her to tell the teacher. Instead I was nice to Big Pam. Since then, there have been too many Big Pams I was nice to because I was afraid.

Postpartum
Journal entry

I was one of those women who ignorantly thought before I had my son that this was something that only affected wealthy, weak, white women who were used to being pampered and didn't know how to handle stress. Let alone the responsibility of taking care of a newborn baby. Then in November 97 I had my own child. A beautiful boy. Uraeus. Those thoughts changed and then I understood. I guess for me the best way to describe it was having all of my fears that I did not want to give voice to in the past...surfacing. Fears that were both realistic and unrealistic. I went through periods of incredible depression. I don't know why. There are plenty of excuses for spending a lot of time sad, not eating, eating too much, crying, contemplating living and dying, but to pinpoint one why...who knows? My son's father and I were breaking up. I didn't have a lot of money. I didn't know where I was going to live. How was I going to take care of my baby? Would I be a good mother after all? Blah blah blah. Just so many things. These were issues I stressed out about. I read that women who recently had babies went through this sometimes and there were cases when it has lasted up to four years. Please God not me. Not four years. But it wasn't supposed to happen to me because I'm...me? Right?

Once I was riding with my family to Las Vegas to celebrate my father's birthday. Along the way Uraeus' milk had spoiled. He was a small baby and was sleep most of the way. I didn't even notice the milk until we got to the hotel. I started to feed him and cried and cried and cried. Everything was wrong and awful about me because the milk was spoiled. I was a horrible mother. I would never be able to take care of my son. I couldn't even keep a relationship going. I was this and this and that after miserable, pitiful that. I know that none of this was true. Ok, I just cannot resist being corny here. I was crying over "spoiled milk." Of course it was more than the milk. So many stories going on in my head it's almost funny now.

During the period I was home taking care of my infant I was also taking care of my friend's twins (yes I said twins) who were only a month older than my son. Why was I doing that? Well now I don't really know. That superwoman thing about us I guess that won't let us say "no." (That's right Jaha; keep blaming it on something outside of yourself.) We lived in the same apartment complex and her boyfriend had to work and my "boyfriend" was at work, and she worked. I wasn't "working" at the time so that made me available to keep her twins. Right? Well no. Sure I had outlets, the church, mother, sister, cousins, friends, but I certainly wasn't using any to deposit my feelings of stress. I held so much inside. Once an old friend called me and started early in the conversation dumping her troubles on me. Special note here, it is best, I think to ask if someone is emotionally ready to handle it when you feel like dumping. I interrupted her when I found a break in her venting and told her that I had been feeling really sad and was experiencing depression. Someone told me, though, that I wasn't qualified to diagnose myself as being depressed because that is a medical term, and I am not a doctor. I went along with it but it doesn't sound right to me because diarrhea is a medical term, and I know when I have it. Anyway, she cut me off quickly and told me that it was all in my head and I should just let it go. What did I have to feel sad about? I had a new baby, right?

Perhaps what I had never articulated clearly enough was that I was never sad about my baby. I was completely in love with him. I was sad and depressed because...I was. And I needed someone to listen to me. Just listen. Not fix it. Not tell me to get over it. And certainly not tell me that my feelings were common and many women felt like that after having a baby. (I don't think I could have handled knowing that I was a regular woman at that time.) Looking back, the person I needed to listen to me the most was me. My body would scream out to me "take a walk!" "Stop taking

on other responsibilities!" "No, you can't baby sit today!" "No, you can't stay up all night listening to her problems!" So it makes sense to me that if I wasn't even listening to myself, then I was sending a clear message to everyone else. I don't know when I stopped feeling like that or what happened. I didn't take anything. I
just, made a different choice. I had everything I needed in my life. I was healthy and so was my son. I had family who loved and supported me, even if they didn't "understand" me, which in retrospect made their love and support even more special. So, what happened? I got involved in my life. Did that mean that I wasn't sad anymore? Nope. It just meant that when those feelings came I chose not to let them occupy my headspace for too long. I began to notice my danger times. If I stayed "down" for over two days it would become difficult for me to get out of it. Whatever it was. I found beauty in the simple things like taking a walk. My precious walks. I still take them.

I was twenty-two and the man I was...in love with? called me a "stupid bitch." And maybe I was one because all I said in return was "I ain't stupid!"

Time

Take me back
Take me back
Take me back, dear Lord
To the place
Where I first received You

Today I visited the church I grew up in. Against the folkways of
the dress standard, I wore dashiki and blue jeans. This has been a
year of confounding emotional backs and forths and I, to my own
bewilderment, longed to feel the sweet breath and look into faces
of folks who have known me from baby shoes to press n curls
and training bras. Have loved me with praise tongues and stern
voices and forgiveness. Rubbed my belly when I was pregnant.
Stood with me. Agreed with me and believed in me. I went to
church. The church that was white with rugged cross and red
steps. I used to love red steps. The church that kindly held my
clouded prayers from when I first understood praying. Not just
on my knees with hands clasped on communion Sundays in
white dress and before dinner, but pray all the time. For
everything. Good grades. New Barbie. Skateboard. For everyone.
For my father, whom I admired but came home drunk early in
the morning and did not notice me waiting by the door with my
arms wrapped around my shoulders and head on my knees to
clean up his vomit before my mother woke up. For my mother
who was fascinating in the way she tried to mask living under
more pressure than she may never be willing to discuss. For
myself, that I would one day have a voice commanding enough to
speak the world of my dreams into fruition. Though I did not
have language yet grown up to divulge all of my narrative, I knew
He was listening. I knew that God had *the whole world in His*
hands. In His hands. He's got the whole world in His hands. And
hands so big still somehow fit into me. 710 south, exit PCH east.
Church. Where there was my Sunday school class that began at
9am and was held in the choir stand behind the pulpit. And Bro.

Rentie picked us up in his station wagon. In the early years the blue and wood brown one, then the fancy burgundy one with air conditioning, teaching us how to oppose the persistent machinations of the devil the whole trip. My youth choir where I was the president for four years in a row and could not sing a note, but was there every Sunday and knew the books of the Bible from Genesis to 1 Corinthians. On second Sundays after we sang in church we went to Bel Vista Convalescent Hospital and sang for the patients and staff. Where I was tall and skinny with long pressed braids and paten leather shoes and fold down socks with white lace on the edges. I wore my first pair of Leggs B coffee grown up stockings from the plastic egg wrapping and my hair down for the first time at that church. Thick and tight curls from the small yellow sponge rollers that absorbed the excess hair grease that Aunt Ruth made and prayed over in her kitchen. There were Easter speeches and Vacation Bible School classes and gospel concerts, prayer and usher board meetings and other weekly and monthly routines that made our church. Home. The church that held it's own
on the KDAY and crip infested streets of 17th and Lemon Ave. in Long Beach very close to my old apartment on Walnut. I lived in Compton before that but I was much too young to remember. My church. I am still a little girl where all the world is mine. My mother still attends. And like my grandmother before her, is the church secretary along with Sis. Birdie King who is my mother's very good friend. And is mighty in a way that I bet Harriett Tubman was, with dark knowing brown eyes that can see the world from wherever she stands. Mostly it was good to see my mother in her element, in her usher uniform, lavender skirt and jacket with white top and scarf and q tip white gloves that you do not dare rush past without private permission, and soft and divine on her tan skin and smooth, short gray hair and authentic grin. Of twelve children she has too readily accepted the role as quiet daughter of the round brown skinned short jolly woman who was sassy and kind. But she is more than daughter. More than water and quiet, than thunder and forgiving. I started to cry

watching her march around the church after the offering to the sharp corner turns and staccato of "We. Are. Sold. Iers." I used to be an usher. Stood knock kneed, long and lanky in the center isle with my back to the pulpit facing the front doors. Left arm behind my back with fist closed and right arm at my side ready to show the parishioners to their seats. But I was not my mother. I did not really care if the saints received a fan or not. Was not concerned if the programs were folded evenly or no. Mostly it mattered to me that I was president of the Jr. Usher Board too. How long will I have her? I wondered. How blessed I am to even know such a woman, whose gloves I could never fill. But with her comprehensive eyes and face. With her buoyant spirit, steady feet and unpolished toe nails that keep moving through it. This is my mother, who is soft spoken and perfect. Who is strong and giving and unknowingly admired by so many. I sat next to a woman who reminded me of my grandmother, Omega Davis, Sis. Davis as she was called at St. Mark Baptist Church. But she was not my grandmother. Had her brown eyes and good skin and outdated Jheri curl and was a pretty woman like her. But she was not my grandmother. Did not have her must be jelly cause jam don't shake like that belly laugh that made the smallest joke even funnier, did not pass me fire stick candy during service or write notes in perfect cursive that made me laugh and were always inappropriate. My grandmother was a wise woman whose every prediction came true.

"Y'all gon see after I'm gone." After she was gone, we saw. She was our Orsen Wells and we did not even know it. Would not even know it. I listened to the pastor preach and his message was on the birth of Christ as it is today the Sunday before Christmas. Bishop Higgins is a handsome man and sharp dresser. Fancy shoes and preacher voice accompanied by organ and electric guitar. You are moved by this man who is the father of six boys and one girl. A husband to Evangelist Higgins who wears beautifully the earmark of preacher's wife and earth mother. Next week they celebrate their wedding anniversary and he asked her to stand so that he can dote over her. Beautiful. I don't know them really. But I am comfortable here as He tells stories of once having very little money but God blessed him to provide a home for his family where there was love and good times amid the absence of material bling. The Higgins family is still new to St. Mark, perhaps only five years now. A family with volumes of history of family and people and places in a church with a catalog of its own.

Bishop Higgins, this great man with the prevailing voice that comes from the bottom of his abdomen, whose potent message is ever inspiring and entertaining at the same time, is not my pastor. Not the Reverend Henry Ford I grew up with since before I was born. The
Rev. Ford that called my mother who did not have a husband and told her where she could pick up her new tire that was already waiting. He noticed hers was bald and did something about it. Rev. Ford knew us like that. No, this man looked at me when he led the benediction as if I were a visiting sinner looking for Jesus who was not lost. He does not know me. Did not know my grandmother, never met my grandfather. Bro. and Sis.
Davis, a couple with twelve children. The Davis's were one of the three big families at St. Mark. The Croom's and Harris's were the others. Bishop did not know us growing up. Time has not allowed him to know most of us. Bishop may not know that Sis. Bass' three sisters died from breast cancer and when she is not smiling, maybe she is just missing them. Maybe even it is the pure integrity of Sis. Bass that smiles only when she is really pleased. The Higgins family was not here when Adrian Dugas surprisingly died, at twelve. Maybe it is not easy for Bro. and Sis. Dugas to sit through the Christmas program where their only daughter who was well spoken and polite would know every line of her
speech. While we understand that he appreciates the warm cloth, he does not know the private stitching of our tapestry. Our quilt that is not secret, but well used and stained just a little. Perhaps

we have not paused long enough to realize that we do not know his. That
he has a story absent dossier and resume of good deeds. Has an award worthy yesterday that we cannot Google or confirm. That maybe the acclimating is rough polishing at times for everyone.

Where did the time go and who were these people I used to baby-sit for fifteen dollars a night and why were they driving and had children of their own? At thirty-six I am not old enough to wonder where all of the time went. These were the same walls and chairs, different choir robes and pews, but same piano and drum set as before. Only time changes, I was beginning to understand. Even the people were not the same. There were too many funerals and birthdays and communions and weddings and funerals so fast here. Too many people I knew eulogized right here on different carpet but same hymns. How will these children survive, I wondered, without Sis. Lang praising every off key song? Without Rev. Roberts who was tall and pigeon toed and had an afro curl and was grown up and child like with us. And we understood him and loved him. He let us call him Bubba. Though most of us knew better. How will service ever really begin without Bro. Lang leading the devotion in his deep dark skinned bass voice with the old Negro 100's? "Bread of heaven, bread of heaven, feed me till I want no more" and the church would respond "Breeeeeeeeeeaaaaaadd oooouuuvvvee heeeaaavveeeen feeeeeeeeiiiiieeed me till ahhhhhhhhhhhhhh waaaaaaaaaaaaaaooooont nooooooooohhhoo mooooooooooreeeeeee."
Then bowing to one knee with the other deacons we would listen to Bro. Crews pray his signature prayer of "Aint gon study war no mo." And my grandfather who smoked and knew the gospel perhaps as well as Matthew or Paul and with common sense to boot and right in every fight, would follow his prayer with one of his own spoken so softly that we could not hear. "I wasn't speaking to you" was his only reply. And if one knew better one did not pursue the conversation. And one always knew better.

There are memories right here on these floors behind these doors that are pieces of me like cells and lashes and pinky toes. That feel good like rent paid and stretch jeans. And hurt at the same time like sore feet and friendships gone bad with no completion and misunderstandings between lovers. There was Vidette and Cheryl and Pam and Cordelia and Kim and my own Aunt Janice who were women I looked up to. And I would be amazing like them when I grew up. There were the Harris sisters whose voices could match a team of angels hands down. And Lezette and Sophia who were always as sophisticated and as beautiful as their names. Sophia, who was only gorgeous. Whose life to me was flawless. Sophia, Sophia, Sophia, who told me the Sunday before her suicide that I was a pretty girl. And there was Nameless who was strict and respected and had a nice house and dutiful wife and new car and his tongue touching mine too many times in a way I was too young to understand and too scared to tell. Again. I suspect now, that I was not the only one. There are pieces of my shaping that have escaped the surface of my recollection, but the bricks, and strips of caulk, and boards of plaster of this building will always know.

I found out that Minnie Sadler was living in a retirement home. A retirement home?
Ma
Minnie?
Yes, even Ma Minnie was older, though she did not look it. It was so good to see her again. At ninety-five she still ranks as one of the best looking women I will ever have the pleasure to know. Dressed from head to toe in short skirt with matching jacket and soft white nylons and red shoes that were haute couture and far outside a ninety-five year-old woman's knowledge. But she knew. She sat proud in her wheel chair under her church hat with red feathers and shiny wig and bag of chocolate candy in hand to give to the children as she has done for forever. She gave some to me. There was the time, I thought. Right here in Ma Minnie's bag. And though my diet does not include chocolate

peanut butter cups I did indulge. A moment sacrosanct with me, Ma Minnie and time that was found and embraced and secretly begged to stay. But time does not. Ever, I drove home slowly, noticing how the city has changed and stayed the same. I called my son Uraeus who is in Bakersfield right now enjoying his father. I told him that I had chocolate peanut butter cups from Ma Minnie and I would send them to him because these were special. But he does not know Ma Minnie, or Rev. Ford, or my grandmother. Only knows stories of my grandfather whom he is so much like. Does not know Bro. or Sis. Lang. Has never ridden in the church bus with Bro. Harris or sang badly in the choir. My son does not know time.

Sunday to Market

I feel pretty in open toed shoes and dark socks
Long flowing skirts and tops
I am girl with baldhead and too long and dirty denim overalls
with platform flip-flops
Daisy behind my ear bag strapped across my shoulder
Wrong shade lipstick on smile full head high
I am beautiful on my way
210 bus on Crenshaw and Vernon
Take a long time to come
I pull out sunglasses and lemon vitamin water
Fried chicken wrapped in foil
Listen to brothas play drums in the park
Watch the sistas dance
Everybody and everything is talking to me
I hear them all at once
Street corner preachers tryin to save my soul
Each one louder than the other
If they would stop talking just a minute
They would see
I'm already saved

Spring

Sorry fall easy
Tears was last to come
Sad been long time company
Not good friend
But loyal
Constant tongue to negate my truth
Can't blame sad for just wanting some attention
We all want to be taken notice
Sad aint no different
Just more persistent sometimes
Is all

Emergency Shelter

I worked in an emergency shelter for women and children fleeing domestic violence.

During the time I worked there I constantly had a cold or whatever. Doctor said it wasn't nothin'. Me, I know it's because the stories kept building inside of me. Calling me to let them out. These notes are about some of the clients and cases. The names have been changed to protect the...

KEISHA, KEISHA, KEISHA

October 2004
Part one

Keisha was a three-year-old grown up black girl who was from Lake Charles, Louisiana. Chocolate skin, three ponytails, barrettes (all the time barrettes), smart mouth and picture booth pretty. One day she was in the play area over by the steps playing house.

Me: Keisha, what are you doing over there?

Keisha: Cookin' greens. I got all this to do before Tonya 'nim come over tonight.

Keisha, in disgust threw down the pretend spoon and stormed over to Michael, a two-year-old white boy from Arkansas who barely spoke. Michael was playing basketball.
Keisha: (completely in his face) Look, I been in the house cookin' all day n workin' hard'n carryin on and you out here shootin' baskets like it's the business! Whatchu think this is? Huh?! Whatchu gon do?

Michael: Teacher!?!?!

Part two

Keisha was sitting at the arts and crafts table with Michael and Tony, a Mexican three-year-old boy from Tijuana. Keisha dealt them the playing cards. Michael and Tony were "counting" them and throwing them across the table. Keisha, on the other hand, had her cards fanned out as if she was a professional card player.

Keisha: I got two books, whatchu got?
Part three

Keisha and Michael were racing the toy cars. Michael had the red one and Keisha had the blue one that kept coming in a distant second. Michael went to the restroom and when he returned his truck was gone.

Me: Keisha, do you have Michael's car?

Keisha: No, his car got towed.

PLAYING HOUSE

Randy and Theresa are brother and sister aged three and four, respectively. They came to the shelter with their mother Becca mid October 2004 from Texas. They showed up in the middle of the night with...stories...from Dallas to Los Angeles all over their faces. It takes a special kind of person to work in domestic violence shelters I found. I also found out that I don't seem to be one of them. I spent almost the whole time I was there trying to save everybody. And I mean everybody. Donating my clothes to the women, some of my son's clothes to the children, working more overtime than was healthy for me. Those women and those children became like part of my family. Just as quickly as they would come, they would leave. On that same middle of the night bus. No goodbye. Just gone. Becca, Randy and Theresa left like that. One day Randy and Theresa were playing "house" in the back yard in the children's area.

Randy: Theresa, you git your fuckin' ass in this damn house you fuckin' bitch!

Theresa: What do you want you fuckin' asshole?!

Randy: What do you think I want you bitch?! My fuckin' food on the table you stupid whore!

Theresa: I didn't have time to cook no food today, asshole!
At that point Randy locked Theresa out of the house and pretended to throw all of her clothes out.

Me: Theresa, come here, sweetheart.

Theresa: What?! You black, fuckin' nigger bitch!

November 8, 2004
Journal entry

I came into work this morning not knowing what to expect.
Karmen called me last night and told me that two clients had left
and two more had come in. Both new ones had babies under two
years old. I was sad to hear that the two families who left were
my favorites. Monica, Mexican, fifty-four, with four children,
Hector sixteen, Annalisa thirteen, Lucia twelve, and Junior nine.
All very bright and had witnessed way too much
for their young lives. Especially Annalisa who had too many hats
to wear. Mother to her siblings and often even to her mother,
daughter, friend, cook, disciplinarian, teacher, translator, and up
until about two weeks ago, wife to her father. I knew that it was
only a matter of time before the house would be too much for all
of them. The women in the house tend to gang up on the new
families, especially the ones that don't speak English. Bullying
them into kitchen duties, taking their money and other
belongings, picking on their children. Some fight back, some
don't. Many leave deciding that it was easier being on the streets.
Sometimes it is.

Today the team had its weekly meeting. We discussed some of the clients in the house. I was a little nervous about this particular meeting because we discussed one of the clients I had grown pretty attached to, Monica. She has five children, Martin 17, Lupe and Lola 15 and Michael and Ricardo 3. She is a kind woman with bright children but she is "low functioning" (according to her files) and makes very poor judgments. I don't like those titles. We had to decide whether or not we were going to let her into the transitional home. Transitional homes are apartments where the clients with children get their own apartments. The single mothers share apartments. It's a good deal because the women get up to two years to get their lives together and get a place of their own. They can even, and are encouraged to work. The monthly rent they pay is based on their income. And at the end of two years when they are ready for their own apartments, they get the money back. Many don't make it, but some do. Anyway Monica. She is a 45-year-old woman who dresses and tries to look like a 16-year-old girl. She has never had her own place with her children. They have lived in shelter after shelter after perverted uncle after shelter after another. She has not been very compliant with the case plans in the different departments we have. I want to vote that we accept her but I don't want her to get into the apartment and then continue being noncompliant with the rules and get herself and the children put out. I don't want to put that out there. She will succeed. She will succeed. She will succeed. She reverts to this baby, baby girl when she is uncomfortable. Which was today at the meeting before the team. She came in wearing this soft pink terry cloth jogging suit and had her bleached blonde hair up in two ponytails and pink and blue butterfly pins. She had on pink lipstick and blue eye shadow. She was even sucking on a lollipop. And then there were the blue contacts. One night I saw her getting ready for bed without all of that...stuff on and I barely recognized that beautiful woman sitting on the couch reading her book. "I'll do whatever you want me to do. I promise I won't be noncompliant again. I promise." I was just waiting for the extended "pleeeeeeeeeeeeeeeeeeeeeeeease."

"I'm really sorry. I'm trying to get my life together. I'm trying to get a job and take care of my kids and everything." This is a woman who hasn't worked since the eighties. I want her to do well.

Staff: What do you plan to do as far as work?

Moncia: I want a good job, you know? A real good one. I don't wanna be working at no McDonald's or Wal-Mart or nothin' like that.

Not what they wanted to hear.

HOLIDAY?

Toward the middle of November one of the clients came to the house after curfew drunk.

It just so happened that Karmen, an off duty staff member was there. If she had not been there, Mary a very petite, older, staff member would have been on duty alone for those two hours. Cathy was very surprised when she found out that Karmen was there. We noticed that the clients would take advantage of Mary because they felt that they could intimidate her. And they did. Karmen wouldn't let Cathy in the house that night and Cathy got loud. Really loud. We were already having problems with the neighbors not wanting us to be there. Cathy, drunk or not knew what she was doing.

Karmen let her in and escorted her up to her room to get her things and told her that she was going to have to leave the house that night. Whatever your state of sobriety, you're not punking Karmen. Five feet ten, thick, social worker, black woman who knew all the

tricks of shelter living. While Cathy was packing her belongings and Karmen was distracted, another client unlocked the back door while another one went to the kitchen and got a knife and pulled it on Mary.

Mary had been being taunted a few weeks before that time and that incident seemed to be in the works. The police were called and Mary wasn't hurt. Just scared. I had hoped that there would be easy resolution to this. Easy meaning, one I wouldn't cry about for weeks.

Some of the women had been approved for transitional homes. Monica and her children were one of the families. This would be the first time they had ever lived in an apartment by themselves. Ever. Well, the house directors had a meeting and decided, three days

before Thanksgiving mind you, that they would clear the whole house. Yes, everyone had to go. The families who had been

approved of transitional homes too. All of them had to find other shelters to go to, family members who would take them in, go back on the
street, whatever, just had to go. All of this would happen the next day. I knew this and tossed and turned the whole night. I had grown attached to the children
and some of the mothers. They were bright and just needed a chance. Just needed someone to acknowledge them as people, unique, loving, people. In the children's
program the next morning, instead of adding glitter to the Thanksgiving Day cards, we packed up their belongings. I cried the whole way through. I was holding onto babies as mothers one by one snatched them out of my arms screaming at me as if I had everything to do with what was happening. "Gimmie my muthafuckin baby! Bitch!" I think I was
"Bitch!" at least a few times every day. How do I turn over a child to someone screaming at me for her "muthafuckin baby" and had no place to go? But I had to. When the children left I sat in my chair crying and praying. Then Lupe, Monica's fifteen-year-old daughter walked into my office. Just sat there. No tears. You thought a sad, crying teenager was something to see, try a one who had cried out all of her tears. She looked at
me. I told her that I had nothing to do with it and how sorry I was. As if that helped. Lupe was such an incredible writer and had a story that would inspire anyone.

Before they moved to that shelter they, the five of them were living in a car downtown Los Angeles. She would do her homework in the middle of the night while her family was sleeping. She said that she got her stories from staying up late and watching the crack addicts out of her "bedroom" window. Her bedroom window that was the front seat of the car parked downtown. Then she would go to school and get picked on by the students and some of the teachers. I didn't know what else to say to her. I asked her to promise me that she would not stop writing. Again she looked at me. Then slowly she told me that two days before that was one of the happiest days in her life. She went to Target with her family and they bought a broom, a mop and two pots for their apartment that they would be moving into just three days away. Their first apartment. No more perverted uncles, no more living in cars, no more shelters, their place. And then this. "So, no" she said, "I can't promise you that I will keep writing. But I do promise you and cross my heart that I will never be homeless again. Even if it means I have to go to jail."

She hugged me, wiped my tears and left.

Ancestor Journal Entries
One of the many journals that I keep is a collection of letters to my ancestors.

Sunday, July 28, 2002, 7:00am Buckingham Rd., Los Angeles

Grandma

Today concludes the Davis Reunion 2002. You would be happy to know that Therman showed up as we were all at yours, Granddaddy's and Bubba's gravesites. He looked good too. Bobbie showed up yesterday at the picnic near Herman's house. Naa was there too along with all of the new babies. Ursula is married now and has a daughter, Madison. Angela and her husband (Michael) and son (Preston) were there. Mike and Cynthia have a second son, Mason. We all had such a good time swimming and playing games and eating and meeting family we didn't know. I met Alan's son Joshua. We are going to St. Mark this morning. Roshann is going to preach.

That was the last time anyone in the family saw Therman. We never heard from him again. No one knows what happened. He stayed with me that night. We talked the whole night away. He slept on a chair next to my bed and we told stories and remembered,
together. He flew back to Atlanta the next day. Later he packed a bag, walked past his wife and disappeared. This is 2006 so that was four years ago.

Red

A friend of mine called me and told me about her daughter's Red party. Like perhaps many of you I had not heard of a Red party before and was sure I had not had one. Curious as to what I had been denied, I inquired. Come to find out, a Red party is a celebration for a young woman who has just started her menstrual cycle. Seemingly, much like a birthday party, there is no set way in which it has to be done. She told me that at her daughter's party the young girls who had not started their cycles wore white dresses and were the hostesses. The women who were still getting their monthly cycles wore red and the women who were not getting their cycles anymore wore black. At her party there was only one woman in black, her grandmother. Each woman gave a few words of advice and encouragement to the honoree and also a gift. The gifts were things like Hello Kitty clear zip bags that held pads, travel sized lotion, deodorant, carmex and other don't leave home withouts. Some of the advice was how a young woman should take care of herself by adding a little vinegar to her bath water during that time and special notices as to the changing moods and body temperatures in the body of a young woman as opposed to a little girl. According to my friend, Sandra, she received as much if not more from the party than anyone. This was as much a celebration for the mother as it was for her daughter. It was a time of accepting that she is not rearing a little girl into young lady hood but a young woman into womanhood. Don't we want our babies to just stay babies? Hearing about this party was very inspiring to me as I thought about the chance it gives young ladies the opportunity to view this part of their lives as something special and not "The Curse." Young women can be encouraged to take this time to be still and listen and know. God speaks to us all of the time and for me the messages are crystal clear during my period. I am sensitive to everything around me. Mostly I am more sensitive to how I am feeling. What's really going on with me. Me. I was eleven years old when I started my period. It was about 2:00 am, which is the time it usually shows up even to this day. The cramps were the most pain I had ever experienced. I used to suffer from very extreme cramping. I believe that everything that is going on in our bodies has something to do with something we are not paying attention to within us. In my case there were so many things I had not said out loud. So many secrets

I was holding onto. It was those secrets that were causing the severe cramping. I didn't realize this and did like most women did and just medicated the pain. I medicated the pain with Tylenol and more silence. The Tylenol put me to sleep and the silence kept the cramps coming. My medicating expanded to Tylenol pm and a glass of merlot. Ok a couple of glasses of merlot and more than a couple of Tylenol pm. There, I said it.

Not that I was ready to do anything about it. I held onto stories and collected more of them because like attracts like. As each thing would happen I would fall into my familiar groove of silence. I knew that it was not serving me but it was how I knew to handle life when it hurt. Be a good girl. Be quiet. Be nice and make people like you, and it would go away. Of course I had not seen it happen but thought maybe it might. It had to.

These days I am much more vocal. Not so nice all the time. Not so important that eeeeevvvveeerrrryyyyboddy like me allllll the tiiiiiimmmmee plllleeeeeeaaasee. Although sometimes it is very easy to fall into my comfortable fuzzy slippers of silence, (and nice

just to be liked). I have noticed the direct correlation between me expressing myself, an action I call living my life out loud, and the cramps I have every month. Of course there is my diet. My diet also has much to do with my silence. When I am eating often I am not feeding my hunger. I am feeding my stories. The ones nagging to get out. They get real hungry late at night when there is no one to talk to. These stories, they talk to me and convince me not to write or talk or paint. And they are very convincing. Somehow, I find myself with ice cream and the remote control and Nick at Nite. Really, it's not my fault. Not me. Not me. It is so much easier, not better for me, but easier to go to bed full and sleepy than it is to be fully present to what is really going on. I get...tired sometimes, you know?

It would be nice if was just that easy. To blame cramps and eating too much and not following my passion on...voices and stories that just won't let me write and paint. The reality, we all know, is that we are not fully present and living powerfully in every moment because, and get this, we choose not to. At least, I chose not to. When I became present to the fact so much of my life was based on the choices I made, I gained so much power. Right then, in that moment. I could exercise, or not. Could eat right, or not. Could engage in stressful conversations, or not. Could release stress though art, or not. Could live, or not. I could suffer and blame it on something outside of me, or live my life powerfully. I could complain every month when my period comes, or I can be still and listen to messages that come, and love myself through it.

Rent

Two birds
Resting at my window
Enjoying the day
Like they got good gossip to catch up on
With each other and all
Two birds
Resting at my window
Clouds are gray
Everybody got sense
Know it's about to rain
They are resting
Don't even seem to care
The first is just a couple days
Away

My son is living with his father this year to go to school. He's spending his breaks and summers with me. Manhood training we're calling it. Too many black boys don't know their fathers. This is a good thing. I keep telling myself. We talk on the phone everyday and write letters often, it's not the same. It's not supposed to be. He's growing up. Though I have covered him with kisses and squeezed him with my hugs, I wish I held him more. But there is a line, I know, between being the mommy who loves and the mommy who does not let go.

Dedication

I failed geometry in the tenth grade and Mr. Brown's thin pink lips were stretched cross his face when he handed me my marks. He said I wasn't smart enough to get it. This is to those like me who don't give a damn about the Mr. Browns and what they think cause we know way better.

After 5

He wonder why she not pretty like she used to be
But he don't see she aint got time for cute
And that's what make her sexy

Confessions

Brothas who so easily
Call sistas bitches
Seem to be the ones who act
Just like them

To my mother on her birthday

It comes most in the dark of morning
The remembering of stories you never had to tell
Truths about daddy I would find out soon enough anyway
Or not
Luxuries you could not afford
Because he gambled the check away sometimes
He chased women sometimes
What you had to swallow
Hearing us cheer as he came through the door each night
Each night that he came
Daddy's home!
Daddy's home!
But where were your cheers
I don't remember your cheers
The ones for you
For you!
Not even in my remembering
I don't remember your cheers
For what it says now
I'm sorry
Even for my remembering
I'm sorry
I remember once he tore up your shoes
Right there at the kitchen table
That did not match its chairs
Amidst our screams
Daddy stop!
Daddy please stop!
Your brown wooden heeled woven shoes
So that you would have to buy yourself a new pair
Yourself
Not a brand new black baby Tabitha
That would tell me she loved me
As long as I pulled the string

As long as I didn't pull too hard
Not a toy whatever for Roshann
Who had to have something
Because I got something
And it's not my birthday either
And that's not fair right?
I was mad at him with you for that
Today I remember it his highest act of love for you
The other good that came from
Schlitz malt liquor and Mary Jane
Our lives are so parallel
Yours and mine
Like you
I didn't know that I was beautiful
He told me I was pretty
And sometimes I believed him
The random hims
The ones that came and went
From you I know that I was smart
A smart girl
You made me believe that I could write
That someone would hear my stories
You gave me that
You learned to fry chicken
So that you could teach me
Because black girls should fry chicken, right?
We stood there in front of 70s style green stove
On brown and white linoleum diamonds
You, really wanting to finish building the bookcase in the den
Me wanting to practice my cursive
I do not like chicken
You taught me lessons bigger than frying
Bigger than black girl chores
I watched you and I became woman
I sat in the hallway on brown and beige shag carpet
Leaned against red leather Britannica encyclopedia set

I watched you in the bathroom
That I helped you paint baby blue
Only in my remembering
I do not recall ever holding the brush
I stared at the tight curls that formed your high afro
Watched you put on black eye liner
And soft Maybellene red lipstick
You were so beautiful
I wanted to look like you when I grew up
I wanted that nose
That was round and sharp at the same time
That could always smell a lie
Those lips...that smile that forgave
Always forgave
Perfect lips
My remembering says
I did not want mine quite so perfect
I do remember that very clearly
And your shoulders
I did get your shoulders
Those shoulders that seem to carry the world
Why do we do that
Carry the world
Nobody asked us to
But we do
I never told you that you were beautiful
We were not mushy women
We were smart girls
I do not remember your kisses
Rather I do
I remember your kisses
Nervous each one like a first date
They came on birthdays and mothers day
And Thanksgiving after prayer
I understood then that you were not huggy and kissy
Neither was your mother towards you

We are shoelaces
You and me
Coming in and out of holes
Twisting knotting up
Wrapping into pretty bows
Holding on tight
Coming apart
Wrapping up nicely again
You made it look easy
The tying and untying
I know that it wasn't
It couldn't have been
You must have extended your prayers each night
After you got up from your knees with me
Long after I was sleep
As I do now with my own child

A boy
One boy seven years now
Not two girls
Just four years apart
Children should not know our prayers
When they are children
They deserve at least that
You braided my hair
Before you learned to braid
I was nine and honored with you handy work
Only I didn't know it then
But in my remembering
I am honored
Proud you kept me little girl
The phone was off sometimes
The lights were off sometimes
Not often
But sometimes
There was always however enough money for

Cheerleading uniforms, hot dogs at night games, piano lessons
And press n curls that cost too much
Even for then
Did you think that I did not know
A smart girl like me
Who could not fry chicken
This poem was intended to be haiku
A birthday wish to slip between the gift and card
But a daughter cannot write a haiku
About her mother
Especially a daughter
Who is a writer
The remembering takes over
It has a mind of its own
There is always one more line that must be added
Just as I go into Albertson's to get only Kings Hawaiian bread and
chicken
My son likes chicken
And leave twelve bags full
I wish you kisses on this birthday
We are mushy women
And strong at the same time

And we get to be weak
When we are tired
And always always
We are beautiful
Like fish who keep moving through endless ocean
And fire
And built and burned bridges
And the healing and accepting
The loving of our remembering

Mother's Day

I am at home in McDonough, Georgia. My new home. The opposite coast of my California birthplace. I am in the house that prayer built and God blessed, that faith knew. In the house whose walls I could not touch and floors I could not walk without your generosity. Right now I am sitting downstairs on the couch in front of the window listening to the rain. Trying to interpret the wisdom of the wind as it races through the leaves. They are speaking to me, I feel. It's now early in the morning and I have been up all night. Intentionally. Two cups of coffee, three sugars, one cream. I am thinking. Thankfully thinking. Tonight I am thinking about you.

There is a bond revered I know, between mothers and daughters. Between you and me. Every year I understand more and more about life and love and being a mother. About being a daughter. You taught me that. I am beginning to know that life and mothering is

happening in the space of what is not said. What is not screamed out loud on front porches, not forced with over spanking and under hugging. I thank you for creating a world for me in that space. You have loved your children outside the norms and folkways of the twentieth century standard. You have boldly loved us with all of your knowing. You let us cry when we were sad and laugh when we felt joy. What bigger gift is there, than the space to cry and laugh, you know? Everything was possible because we lived in your world. Your world, that was perfect in all of its imperfections, the way that God planned.

How did you do it? I wonder sometimes how you managed to work and keep a home for us and the many lessons that came, learned and postponed. I only remember you beautiful. Real beauty. The beauty that comes the day after sponge curlers, all tight and

restrained by the rules of this world. But you are a free woman, and taught us to be free. The lovely that comes with not knowing how everything is going to work out. The blessed assurance of

resting in God's hands knowing that He always provides. I can only imagine the faith you had to hold onto. I cannot thank you enough. I know that there were tears that you hid from us. There were worries, I'm sure, that you did not express. Will never, I imagine. There are questions that run amuck in minds of mothers. Did I do it right? Are my children prepared? Did I give them enough? The questions do not end. At least they do not for me. They find me when I am weak. I see them sometimes at every turn. I open cupboards and wonder if I kissed my son enough. In my daily shower I wonder if my discipline on him was too strict or not enough. Am I being who God wants me to be for him? They are temporarily silenced when I take time to love myself. When I take time to breathe, just breathe. To be still and know that God is guiding every step of my journey. I must remind myself, over and over, that God is being God through me. Using my fingers to hold and my eyes to see. Using my heart to love. You know, perhaps I spoke out of
turn. I do not know that these questions run in the minds of all mothers. I only know that they float above my head. I mention this now to free you of doubts you may have ever entertained. I could not have created a better mother. And I am an artist. A very good one I fancy. I am thankful everyday for you. You have sacrificed so much for my needs and desires. You were the handbook I needed. You are the guide that God created for my journey. It is assumed that the mothering ends when the children are grown. This assumption is
even held by the mothers. Living on both sides of the fence I am thankful that it does not. End. I am so blessed right now to be a mother and daughter in tandem. I am also blessed to have you with me, gifting me with your wisdom. You are always on my mind. My heart is bigger my life more glorious because you created that space.

Haiku for mamas with little big boys in public schools

Mamas know what time
It is when they look in the
Faces of they boys

December 31 haiku

Ghetto babies sleep
With mama New Years Eve cause
Guns be going off

Uraeus

I am lying on the living room floor next to my son
5am my hand on his belly feeling him breathe
Kissing his cheek
Watching him dream

I dated a man once who told me that I'm not who I think I am. I think his issue is that I am even more than that.

And so here I am

In the space of me finding myself
Have been right here all the time
Lips poked and too silent
Full and too afraid to kiss
Speaking words like cotton
Words like knives to kill / to heal
Eyes wandering and seeing beyond
Always seeing beyond
Constantly missing the gold at my feet
But I see now
Feet being massaged and cemented
Feet flying
Voice red and whispers
Backbone strong and itching
Always the itching
Fight harder to stay longer to be more to loose fear to let go
Fingers writing
Always writing
Words I could not speak
Writing roses and violets
Writing reds and blues
Always the blues
Always the blues
Teeth talking loud teeth saying nothing teeth screaming and
scraping
The back and forth the chewing the up and down
The questions
The words and thoughts
Conversations and quizzes
Fights and frustrations the blessings and lessons
The talking to myself
Often the talking to myself
Always the talking to myself
I am open to the crazies that come sometime

The weirdoes in my head
All me
All me
I am a young girl running in circles
A little baby spinning around
Grown woman grounded and grateful

If

I feel better then I've ever felt
You are always here
And we don't let a day go by without talking
I'm holding you like I don't want to let go
You aint pulling away like you want me to stay
Then why aren't we doing this

The night of the Revolution

Someone had signs
Someone had paint
Someone had a headache
And someone got shot
Someone stopped to rest
Someone pushed forward
The rappers were bought and the poets were scared
But we had our tongues
We would speak for ourselves
He used his shoulder
She used her bag
They used those sticks
And we all used our
Voices
There was fish and pork
Carrots and chips
And everyone ate
Someone whispered and someone cried
Someone lied and someone screamed
Someone shoved and someone surrendered
We were all there
And no one was
Silent

haiku for too black too strong
You don't gotta hate
Everybody else to show
That you love yo'self

Blue Sky
There are women in my head
Belly dancing apricot gyrating women
With long jaw lines and deep green eyes
Feet reaching high above mountain peeks
Scraping toe rings across clouds
Walking upside down around heaven all day
Fingers stretching below into sea graves
Tickling fish fins and secretly signing
Keep moving keep moving
I understand now why
Bridges had to fall for new roads to be built
Backs had to break
For new spines to stand straight
Gumbo and collard green voices
Sing harmoniously with the aki and calilou arms raised high
Held by the Chinese praying women's whispers
I am every woman
Doing the impossible
Continually unfolding into my infinite possibilities
As I release and let go tools of yesterday
That do not serve me
And I am always my highest self
Even when I don't remember
I am a very powerful woman
As God is God through me
Living each moment for the living of that moment
Recognizing that it whatever it is is already all good
I am not okay if you are not well too
I am all the power of water
When you are fire with me
And always always I am beautiful
Time has only loved me
The storms have only empowered me
To conjure more magic
And when I close my eyes

There are satin sheets of purple, turquoise and oxblood
There are blue-black Ghanaian women
Sitting waiting patiently for me to fly
Understand that I am well on my way
There are still stories to be told
I respectfully respond
Babies to be birthed and wars to be won
The ancestors hold me dear and breathe through my pores
And you should not come close
If you mean me any harm
There are big bootied big mamas in me that don't play
And despite what you may see
I am taller than the palm trees
I am working here
Do not mess with me

I don't take the time often enough to honor myself. To sit still and accept that I am a wonderful person on my journey of life and love.

Musings of a black woman going through the change of life everyday

Everyday a black woman going through the change of life

There are things a woman thinks about when she is dying
Don't ask me how I know
She thinks about water mostly
How it tickle your face as it rise above your neck
She thinks about music
Long slow deep southern gospel
No matter where she come from
Or what religion she learn
She remembers the sweet Jesus her grandmother knew
Whether she can hold a tune or no she sing from the bottom of her belly
She finds her tribe with those sounds
Groaning moaning feel good don't feel good make you better healing sounds
Long and drawn out
A dying woman thinks about the times she stood still in life
She remembers the moss and vines growing between her toes
In that moment she is moved to move
She is compelled to live and break free of the chains she tied around her own neck
She know better now
She knows now that safe aint always so safe
Roses aint always so sweet like she thought
A young woman being still and safe might start to think a chokehold is a soft caress
And it aint
A shackle is a shackle
And a kiss is a kiss
But what do young safe living women know
This dying I'm doing is good for me

Lettin be dead my yesterday and walkin big footed into
tomorrow
I don't know what's out there for me
I just trust God to know the world He created
I believe the clouds can hold me like they promise
There are things a woman thinks about when she knows
tomorrow is coming

Tomorrow

I will be an old woman
Living right here in this house
This Georgia sun this Georgia moon
The children will pass
They will point at my porch
Knock on my door for candy, for apples
For love
But I will not have candy
Only stories to tell
Stories for sale
Stories about boys, about girls
Stories about people who lived long long ago
About trees, about birds
Stories about deer
Young women will bring me peas and fruit
Beans and bread
But I only ask for wine.
Red
More wine please
They think, these young fruit bringing women,
That I have secrets to tell
Secrets to make their simple lives easy
So they will be kind to me
Their boys will water my lawn and wash my car
Their girls will sew me dresses and paint my nails
Pink
I don't really wear pink
But they will bring me pink
No wine
Just pink dresses
Clean cars
Cut lawn
Smelly nails
All the time

But I only ask for wine
Red
And time
And for someone to read stories to me
Tell me stories
Don't just take all the time
Stay, I may ask
I will not beg, maybe
Remember James Baldwin, Toni Morrison with me
But they only want my secrets
So that they will live easy
I am a witch, the girls think
I keep women young forever, they surmise
I should have such secrets, I say
I hear it in their jump rope songs

> That old lady at the end of the road
> Got a whole lotta stories
> So I been told
> I brought a bucket full a peas
> And I sat at her feet
> And she passed some good spells
> Onto me
> A one, a two, a three...

Somewhere in the space of my meditation

Today I will see God in everyone I meet
I will speak to everyone as if I am speaking to God
I will talk about everyone as if I am talking about God
I will give my word to everyone as if I am giving my word to God
I will do business with everyone as if I am doing business with God
I will forgive everyone as if God is forgiving me

Water Water Everywhere

Water is healing
Water enhances my dreams
Water cleans my body
Water washes off the day
Water washes off the night
Water is strong
Even stronger that fire
Water is soft
Water is loud
Water is soothing
Water is bold
Water forgives
Water is music
Water is quiet
Water protects
Water provides
Water makes me remember
Water lets me forget
Water helps me relax
Water makes me wonder
Water dares me to be myself
Water lets me use my voice
Water cleans my lungs
Water inspires me to write
Water accepts me
Because of/ in case of/ in spite of
Who I am
Water knows the truth about me
Water loves all of me
Water touches me in places I can't reach
Water reminds me that I am beautiful
Water understands without me having to explain
Water is thankful that I *am*
I am my authentic self with water

I am free to sing out loud with water
Water demands that I be truthful
Water accepts me when I lie
I dance with water
I sing with water

Hair

One night my son said
Mommy I like it
But why do you wear your hair short
I said
So that nothing gets in the way me seeing all of you
To which he replied
Thank you
But if it were long how would you wear it
I told him I would wear it long and pulled back
In a ponytail
Maybe braided or locked
Where I could reach back and swing it
Use it as a weapon if I had to
All to protect you

Spa Divas

Right now I am sitting on a brown leather couch
Slouching really
Comfortable with my laptop in between my legs
I am in the spa on Olympic east of Crenshaw
No one complains that I am typing on my computer in the spa
No one complains out loud
It is most important that I am comfortable
And I am
Everything happens south of Wilshire
On and just east of Crenshaw
You can buy two tacos for under a dollar
From the Mexican street vendor
You can get your car washed for $7.99 on Tuesdays before 9
You can get a blow job and caught up in a drive by
At the same time
Name it and it can happen over here
But this is a space for women
All women
Only women behind these doors
Beautiful women
We are all beautiful
We are all naked under the thin cotton lime green robes
The woman on the couch next to me is telling her friend
That another friend of theirs left her husband
Her friend responds that she knew it was going to happen
And the husband had it coming
In the next breath she warns her friend
To beware of Barbara because she is a bit of a gossip
I find this funny because we never seem to see ourselves in
others
Forty five women are here
For forty five reasons
We are releasing our frustrations and fears
We are relaxing and dreaming

We are daring ourselves to be ourselves
We are breast of all shapes
Thighs of all sizes
Chocolate of every hue

The woman in the sauna
Has had a long day
I assume
She rests her head on the cement siding
I see with each exhale
Every contract
Every coffee break
Every fired secretary
Every male hand and inappropriate touch
She is washing off the day
I think
But I cannot stare
But sometimes we do
Stare
I see myself in these women
All of them
They stare
Because they see themselves in me
Most of the women in here are Korean
I dance to the rhythm of the language
People say they sound angry
But I understand
Black folks are like that too when we get excited
Sometimes they are a bit louder than one should be in a spa
They are just excited I say
They are just excited
They are just excited
And I just keep dancing
Women are so beautiful
Old and young
Gucci and Goodwill

Black and white and Korean and Samoan
There is a bond I think
Between naked women in short lime green robes

Robin's Belly

Robin has secrets hiding in her belly
Robin doesn't want her secrets anymore
Her belly is too big
Robin wants to tell the world
Why her belly is so big
Robin sucked her neighbor's penis
When she was only four
No one wants to hear this story
Robin should just forget
Robin wants to be in love
But Robin is too afraid
Robin settles for relationships with unavailable men
Men too busy with their careers
Men who are not quite over their ex wives
Men who are not quite over their youth
Robin should just understand that men don't want to settle down
Robin is not a housewife
Robin needs to know
That that's what good men want
Robin should just forget
Robin doesn't want to rock the boat
So Robin sends her secrets sailing
She doesn't tell her stories
When they seem too sad
Men don't want to hear life stories
Robin will tell her stories
And someone someday
Will listen and enjoy
Someone someday will understand
Why Robin cannot forget

Dream Notes

I had a dream last night that you were my husband and I was
happy to be your wife. You came home late at night or perhaps
early morning because vaguely I remember a new sun over your
shoulder when I opened the door for you. Why did I open the
door for you?
You were flaunting a folded t-shirt of yours. Just a plain white t-
shirt. So why was it folded so neatly? Why were you holding it so
carefully? What were you so at peace
about? I watched you walk up the steps balancing the t-shirt on
your right palm like a waiter does a full tray. You don't even
wear t-shirts. Not really. I followed you to the bedroom and
asked why you were carrying it and you said without fret or
hesitation because you spent the night at another woman's
house. You even said
her name, though I do not remember it now. You laid on the bed
as if to begin a nap, or watch a ball game after hard days work.
You were at ease while my heart was racing and eyes filled with
fear too scared to water.
My brows plucked perfectly always touched in that moment and
met at the tip of my nose almost. I think.
I asked if you were sleeping with her. And why do we say
sleeping? We are afraid. We are just afraid. The name Vicki
comes to mind. Yes, Vicki. But casually, too casually like sipping
on white wine or blowing smoke from a blunt you said with
shrugged shoulders
"sometimes" and reached for another pillow for your head. You
did not watch me grab my heart in slow motion. Turned over
when my knees became weak and I was sinking to the floor. Fast.
Then, I was not dreaming anymore. I opened my eyes and let the
tears fall and I thought, tears and thumping hearts from Dream
World should stay there? Right? But mine did not. Even now in
my remembering, twelve hours later, sharing you with Vicki did
not hurt as much as you looking away when I fell to the floor.
And then I thought, and this time out loud, the man of my dreams

would catch me if my knees were weak. If he was the man of my dreams.

If/not/who?

Not so much the tension in the chest
Not the shortness of the breath
I've been through this before
The calls I can't complete
The words that I won't say
It's the time that goes so slow
It's the pretending not to know

He/Lover/Partner/Mine

He is my lover and we are friends
More honest, he is my friend and we are lovers
Perhaps he is my forever friend
But he is my for right now lover
At least right now
He is not my perfect partner
The one I pray for
The one I know exists
He is not the one
He is not at least right now
The sex between us is more than good
If I were to compare
He is the best I've ever had
He is gentle and giving
I feel safe in his arms
There is no pressure
There are no worries
I am safe in his bed
Safe the way a child is safe at home
No matter the night sounds
No matter the wind
There is always the mommy
There is always the daddy
For me in his arms
There is always him
I let him kiss me on my vagina
But never on my stomach
My secrets are there I tell him
There inside my belly
I think he understands
But he does not ever ask
I will let my perfect partner touch my belly
I will let my perfect partner hold my secrets
And we will throw them out together

Perfect is as perfect loves
And we will know each other when

Beautiful Beautiful Song

My toes are rarely painted red
My brows not always plucked
My hair not often brushed
My speech not always clean
And I am beautiful
Beautiful beautiful
Beautiful all the ways to be
Yes I am beautiful
Beautiful beautiful
I am who I choose to be
There are circles on my eyes
When I stay up late at night
I get dressed in such a rush
When I have nowhere soon to be
And I am beautiful
Beautiful beautiful Beautiful all the ways to be
Yes I am beautiful
Beautiful beautiful
When I am living out my dreams
And you can be too
If you would just be you

Ruth Forman

What she say so good
In her prayers each morning
Make her peace so still
Do she sit crossed legged
And rest her head
And all that hair twisted over
Those thin brown folded fingers
That must also clutch
The good piece of sky
She is feather descending slowly
In cold Chicago November
And everybody stops still and listens
Even if they way too busy
And got someplace to go
They know Gods voice when they hear it
They know good news when it's comin'

Family Reunion

When I was a young girl
My cousin Angela would come out to California from
Philadelphia
We would stay with her at my grandparent's house in Long
Beach
And play with her
My grandmother had a big mirror in her living room
And I would stand in front of the mirror and comb my hair
I had long hair growing up
Black girl long
Just past my shoulders
Angela said I was stuck up because I combed my hair so much
She doesn't know that I combed my hair so much
Because I never thought I was good enough
I was always fixing me
Each twisted ponytail was an audition for acceptance
Every bang every braid

Musings

Today I heard a gunshot in the alley under my window
I am not wise to the makes and sizes of guns
I am a poet   an artist   a mother
Three shots to be precise
And not just me
Somebody else hadta heard it too
It was three in the afternoon
It was a sunny day   June
These are the things that riot my headspace when I endeavor to write about
Grandmothers   Garvey Drums
My poems are little now
Perhaps someone's life has ended and no one has missed a beat
At the liquor store Crazy Melvin is begging for change
Rolanda the crack head is selling pussy
In unit b Demarco is smoking weed
And the couple downstairs is making love and I am listening
Because it is beautiful
I imagine she lays face downward and grips the headboard tightfisted
While he is stroking inside of her long thick
The cushion of her backside is Christmas   merlot rent paid
The fucking is good
I am never short of stories on Buckingham Rd
An elegant name for a street with such drama
Even more ironic that it intersects King
Yesterday someone pissed in the hallway
The ice cream truck comes by after dark
And last October the brothas set off fireworks starting at one in the am
I would like to blame this on the white man
It is eleven pm and I am up writing because that is what I do
But I am searching for the who of who I am on this Saturday night in Los Angeles

Where someone is being asked to dance
Bishop Collins is preparing his message
And Good Times don't come on local networks no more
Maybe Michael was too black too strong for tv
Thelma too gorgeous to be nappy and brownskinned
And I surmise they killed off James
Because white America couldn't handle
A black man sticking with his family through bad times
I am writing
And the musings and prophecies just come

Like Wednesday before last
The children were out front playing
Two boys and a girl on one side
Three boys to the other
A volleyball type game
Except there was one child in the middle
In my day
        I am old enough to have a day
We called it keep away
Now   Monkey in the Middle
This I believe I can blame on the white man
But life in the hood ain't always bad
Like on Fridays Hank the dealer buys
Books and balloons and toys and food
For the children who don't have very much
And the grandmamas and granddaddies
Are ma'am and sir
And the peace n sage sistas are
Queen and miss ladies
Lil Andre carries the groceries for Mama Jerome
When her boy aint around
But the splendor of moments like these and more
Are shadowed by my neighbor Claire
Getting the fuck beat out of her by her boyfriend
I don't know his name

Every kick follows a stupid bitch this
Every slap a silly muthafucka that
I am so sorry that I cannot make her have a better life
Still my mind wanders
I fancy Leimert Park recalled Little Africa
Where all of the business are black owned
For real this time
The young sistas in training eagerly receive council
On hoochie coochie fryin chicken and bein' grown
While the he soldiers are braided dashikied and employed
It is Saturday night in the jungle and I am just
Writing

What a world
Journal entry

This is the world I live in, and I'm ready to move. Maybe in a year or so this will be a wonderful neighborhood. Right now the gangsters and drug dealers are just too...present. Currently my neighborhood us under regentrification. A strategic plan to change it from black to white. It's too easy to just say that the management company is running us out.
Really, sometimes we out white folk the white folk. The late rent payers were evicted months ago. Now it's just the workers and the gangsters. Frankly, they can have it.

Actually it's not that simple. The rent is good and the place looks ok. But when I look out my window I don't want to see twenty-two people just hanging out, and only three of them are kids. And it's after midnight. I don't want contact high just coming up the stairs to my apartment. I don't want to pass the dope head in the hallway who just bought a rock from downstairs. And every time I open my door, should I hear blaring hip hop coming from another apartment. I'm not saying that good things don't happen in this neighborhood but this is crazy. I look around and I see the management company showing up out of nowhere with paint cans
and push brooms finally cleaning up the place. And we think they're doing this for us.

Oh, you wonder what happens when there are just the drug dealers left? Well, the police finally do their job.
I was speaking with a young man the other day in a coffee shop in Leimert Park. I see him hanging out from time to time. A good kid. A sophomore at Howard University, an artist, and really good. He emails me stories and poems about why I shouldn't leave the ghetto. That I should embrace our people. That every aspect of our community is necessary, even the gangsters. Really? I respond. I know where he's going but I want to hear his

response. He says that their fire is necessary. If there is every a civil war again here in this country then we will need folks on our side who aren't afraid to set it off. He says that their energy is just misdirected, they aren't aware of who their enemy is. I don't know.

Dear Reader

Define yourself...on paper, out loud. Hear yourself say who you are. If you don't know who you are you will believe other peoples definitions of you and that's too much power to give anyone. When we believe other people's definitions of us we wear the labels they give us too comfortably. Well, not so comfortably, but we wear them anyway.

Street life

One:

I was on the corner of LaBrea and Pico one night at the phone booth. Four brothas in a navigator pulled up and the one in the passengers seat rolled down his window and politely complemented me and asked if I had a man. I told him yes and he wished me a good evening. Now the one in the back seat just couldn't seem to leave well enough alone. He rolled down his window and said "Well won't you suck our dicks then." Of course I was offended but I didn't even have to address it because the brotha in the passengers seat turned around and socked him in the chest so hard that I can still hear it today and said " Nigga, you don't be talking to that kinda bitch like that!"

Two:

Two brothas were arguing outside of a coffeehouse one night after a poetry reading (I don't know why that's symbolic here, but it is.) Apparently one had disrespected the other ones woman. "Nigga, why you trippin? That ain't even yo bitch. That's just yo ho.
You know you can't treat yo ho like you treat yo bitch." The other guy was still upset but accepted it like it was written law and acquiesced.

Times

I call myself gon kill myself behind some drama once
But it didn't work
That's ok 'cause I had me a plan
Was gon go crazy next
Leave a note in cursive penned sloppy in crayola
On stretched canvas
Explainin the heavy under my feet
The quick on my tongue
Nervous in my belly
But the phone rang
Alisha can talk all day
So we shot the shit about baby daddies and politics
And a couple of Spike Lee flicks
She say she come up with a new poem and I say good
'Cause I shol needed to hear one
Just like I knew it would it lifted me up the only way
Real good friends could
We reminisced on days when times was worse
I'll admit it I bought the damn thang
With every intention on wearin' that long brown wig and shakin
my ass
If I could just get up the courage
Privately I would be his dancer
Deep down inside I knew that wasn't my answer
I said goodbye
She wouldn't let me go till I changed it to
See you later
She tell me
Mine aint no bigger than nobody else's
The rain don't fall harder
Grass aint no more brown
Sun aint no more hot
And everybody's got to decide if he's gon
Deal with the waves that come

Go on and enjoy the sky
Blue or not
Just hurt so much cause it's mine is all
I read a lot and I know a little
According to the law of rhythm
The measure of the swing to the left
Is the measure of the swing to the right
Based on my own insight
I suppose it's just that I feel the low lows
'Cause I'm continually blessed with the super highs
Knowing this don't make me too wise to break down sometimes
And I cry
Tears for the tired I been of typing forms and scrubbing floors
Slangin' art from beach to beach and cds from sea to sea
And what's funny
Is that what I complain abut one week
The same is my blessing the next
I know that life aint nothing but how you look at it
And from where you looking from
From where Lisha stood
Mine looked all right to her
In the heat of it all
The bruises hurt worse than the roses smell good
Aint that really the struggle
Seeing the rainbow through the smog
And how would you know it was winter
If you never felt the fall
It's all about the goin through it to the getting to it
Real life and bullshit got little to do with karma
As it do the lessons you hear to learn
I understand
So I breathe for a livin'
Because I try not to spiritual lie to myself
I feel my pain when I hurt
And right now
I'm just trying to keep the paint wet on the paper

And the prose flowing flawless in the midst of
Battling for the rent and waiting for the check
Putting half on the gas to put it all on the phone
Holding out for just compensation
With time and family and my mind on my back
About cashin' in on my dreams
In exchange for two weeks paid vacation
You see poetry is a lifestyle
And this is my call
I answer proud knowing that the Most High would provide
Still I'm weak sometimes

'Cause sometimes the quatrains don't rhyme or the haikus too long
The metaphors don't make sense or the gigs don't pay dollars
And you can't write cause the words don't show up
On top of all the other black holes in your soul
You fightin' not to keep
Your little poetry aint all that deep
And that's a heavy for a poet to admit
In the wee hours of the morning after a bottle of hen and white Zen
I flipped that coin
Heads I would stay and play
But come tails
I would pay
So I stepped back and took a look at my hand over some monkey bread
I'm a winner if I play my cards right
And so are you
Times might not come to this if you just allow yourself to admit
That even in the it's all all goodness of it all
It aint ok sometimes
I'm talking to me too
There is one mind and one presence and one God
When you hurt then I do too
But if I aint ok then neither are you
Still I flip
For fun
And tails
Tails
Three out of five come tails
Now I wonder if Ogun and Oshun aint testin' my gangsta
But I stay
Head up back strong through my hustle every day
At the end of it all
Sometimes I wonder who care anyway
I could shoot myself

But then my carpet is beige and the blood will never come up
My landlord is a mean somethin'
Still that's a messed up thing to do to someone
Lisha say I aint ready to go
'Cause my mouth steady movin' with excuses to stay
We talked awhile
I felt good every dollar we run up
It was her dime
So I kept right on till I felt all the way a little bit better
We laughed a good one
My son woke from his nap and together we made
Peanut butter and jelly sandwiches and
Played good guy bad guy till he say
I got you mommy you gon
And I hold him close and say
Sweetdahlin I aint goin' nowhere for
A for real long time

Brian McKinney

The scene opens on an exterior daytime view of an old (California old) neighborhood in Long Beach. Not Snoop and Warren's Long Beach. In fact, it's seventeen and a half minutes northwest of two one and Lewis. The west side, thugly called "the weak side" because the drama, to the naked eye, pales in comparison to the so-called East Side (the video), which is overly congested with multi-family dwellings, barber shops, storefront churches and liquor stores. More, Auntie's and Nana's Long Beach, where housewives still shell peas and barter sugar for apples and watch each other's children and everyone respectfully greets Mrs. Jones whether or not she cares to respond. Indeed, all of this in the crazy '80's, and I, still a child, high school, innocent enough, was unknowingly blessed to bear witness.

At St. Luke's in the daytime, the grounds were well kept and the church secretary's blue Toyota Corolla sat parked in the same spot everyday. Everyday she had coffee and read her favorite passage of Psalms, all in time for All My Children. Then she's began her duties of typing reports on the church's income and expenditures, and on members who had come by Christian experience or those who sought baptism. This was St. Luke's by day, but the moon brought a different vibe. Still does. Spooky. A comfortable familiar however, to those drawn to the underground.

Brian McKinney was one. His moniker was Big Mac. Corny now, but nineteen years ago it was the name to have and Big Mac was the man to know. He could get the goods. Guns. Pussy. Dope. At seventeen and six feet, dimpled and Jheri curled, light skinned (west coast '80's fine), he was well read for a man his age, for a cat with his rep. Big Mac, smooth and a poor decision maker soon to run out on his luck, traits many youngsters possessed was caught...slippin'. He, a Long Beach Crip, had strolled aware and careful in L.A.'s blood land known as The Jungle. Not his first

105

time, still not a habit. This time he was not visiting some chick. Not seeking revenge. Not stopping for gas. This time, per his mother's demands, he was, by bus, visiting his grandmother, who just wasn't ready for him to leave yet. And asked in voice only poets and big mamas and

minister's wives with big hats and round bellies could muster, if he could stay at least until the end of Wheel of Fortune. Please. And he, looking into the eyes that had read Revelations before Genesis was thought, could not say no to her. She wouldn't understand how those "slobs" be trippin'. Slobs? Or that he and Lil Scoops had crazy beef. She would send him to the bus stop well fed with blessed oil on his forehead and prayed over with faith that in the name of Jesus and John Kennedy and Martin Luther King, Jr., he would get to the bus stop unstepped to. Even remain safe until she'd again

see him Thursday after next, if God should say the same.

But, no. Brian McKinney was shot and killed that night by another man and woman's boy. That heavy on his mother's neck, somehow not being enough, today she goes about her days remembering that on the eve of her only child's services, while his body waited alone cold beyond a comforter's cure, his murderer, captured only by karma (maybe), tossed his body, spray painted his casket in red letters, Old English font, now tattooed on

the chest of her memory, fresh until her forever ends. Any why? Over what?

This story is about the courage it takes to look beyond his gang status and see that he was her boy. And always kissed her goodnight. Ate greens with ketchup. Loved fish with his grits. The hole in her heart now is filled only with the comfort in knowing that at least he is safe.

Return to St. Luke's.

By now, everybody knows the routine. Same show. Different star. White roses to contrast the midnight robes. Tears rioting down faces, looting smiles and leaving empty spaces. For some, the air is laced with questions of the fairness of God. For others, near the rear there is a stench of doubt regarding the existence. The preacher tries to preach. The deacon tries to sing. But it all seems for naught, amidst the mother's screams.

A Soldier's Story

There are shadows of ex lovers ablaze in my mind
A team of them
I battle with each one
Individually though
As if somehow they know that
Together they are too much for me
I am thankful for their generosity
Still they wait
Some patiently and some no
All in line
To pick my clothes
Tell me I'm wrong
Yell at me in public
I keep forgetting that public is not worse
I am a wild horse waiting to be tamed
They must think
The lot of them
Sometimes I fight back
Sometimes I do not
I write about them
Then delete them from my files
I am too nice
I change their names to protect their privacy
But I should not
I should warn other women
That he is possessive
He is a crack head
He likes dick
And he can't fuck
But I don't
I keep quiet
But the voices don't stop
So here I am arguing with the ghosts of past dick yesterdays
In my car

Out of the shower
Just before bed
Sometimes after prayer
I must look silly
I think
Fighting with invisible men

Art. Connection. Culture.
Journal entry Tuesday, June 27, 2006

A normal day for me. If normal can be defined at all. Up early. Breakfast. Some television. Today's day included a drive out to City Hall East in Atlanta, Georgia. On the fifth floor of City Hall East is where the Office of Cultural Affairs has its offices. For now at least. I understand that the building has been sold and the Office of Cultural Affairs (OCA) must relocate. As an art lover, an artist, a mother, a new resident of the outskirts of Atlanta, I am paying close attention to this news. But this is not about Atlanta or the OCA, not about art or culture; this is not even about my day, not really, but kinda. On the first floor as I entered the building under the dark parking structure, past the metal detector and police officers, down the long white corridor, was an exhibit called Body Maps which featured ten life sized outlined bodies of nine women and one man. Each body map was a separate painting. The art was colorful which is what first caught my attention. It was childlike and left-handed and honestly brilliant in a Basquiat kind of way. There were some words and phrases written on each painting. Most of the writing was in a South African language. But next to each painting was a literary description of the painting and a bit about the artist/author. I stood
there and the tears were building and building fast. BODY MAPS inspired the book, LONG LIFE, a collaborative book of positive HIV stories of the Bamanani women.
I am usually attracted to art with mothers and babies and red is my favorite color. My attention went first to the painting by Ncedeka. From a distance she could be telling the story of a long day and finally putting her beautiful sleepy baby down to nap. But then something grabs you and demands that you stop and know that there is more to this to tell. Much more. Much more to this exhibit then I was prepped for. Look at me, needing to be prepped for real life. Ncedeka painted a picture of herself holding her baby because she is happy when she thinks of her

baby. Her baby who died in 1999 after only a year and four months on this planet. She became sick. She was told that her baby did not have HIV but her health kept failing. Ncedeka was unknowingly carrying the virus and was breastfeeding her child. She wishes still that she could have more children. Thozama is a young girl whose stepfather beat her and said that he would no longer pay for her to go to school because she had a boyfriend. She went to live with her boyfriend whom she later broke up with because he had twelve other girlfriends. "Always changing, changing, changing." She met another man and married him. Thozama found out that she is HIV positive and believes she contracted the disease from her first boyfriend because "he is getting thinner." Her husband told her that if she goes to find out her status not to tell him because he cannot sleep with someone who is positive. So she did not tell him and they have a child. She has only told the rest of the world. No one else. At Bongiwe's story I had to release the tears that had been building. "I was raped. But I would say I was fortunate because not all of them raped me. The other one hit me with a beer bottle on my head and blood started coming out." And then there is Babalwa who is also HIV positive and has to deal with this daily and lives in a community where so many are sick because of this disease says, "I feel like my life is not finished." Nomawhetu was beaten and stabbed by men trying to rob her and she defended herself by stabbing one of the men.

She tells this story and you know that there are many, many stories she has to tell. But she is living through it. She closes by saying that her sister killed herself. And you just know that Nomawhetu will live through this too. This too? Some of them do not have the drugs available to them that they need but they understand that finding something to be happy about keeps them going as Victoria says "When I get sad, I get sore and I feel the pain all around my heart." Me too, Victoria, me too. Noloyiso remembers her first boyfriend, Babs when she is sad. She loved him and had their baby when she was in the ninth grade. The same year he died. Before he found out she was pregnant. She has had other boyfriends, but it is Babs she misses. Bulelwa was beaten by her grandmother for getting pregnant but her grandmother is there with her everyday to take care of her baby. Grandmothers.

Thobani was the only man in the group. He dropped out. This seems to be how many of the men are dealing with this issue. Not discussing it. He comes to the group when he is really sick, as many men do, but by then it is too late. My tour of the BODY MAPS ended with Nondumiso's story. "If you hear the president saying something you think it's the truth. But here in South Africa the president is not always telling the truth." The president? Lying? Come on now Nondumiso. This was not some newspaper. This was not some campaign for condoms; these were real women who had real lives and real families to feed and real babies waiting for them to get better and feed them and live forever. Forever with a normal life. If again, normal could be defined at all. One woman told of witnessing her own mother dying. She said that she was glad that God took her because there was nothing else she could do to help.

The insides of her bones were showing. So I was standing there, in front of each piece, crying, moving slowly thinking about the four other times I had passed the stories before. I remember walking through the gallery the first time the exhibit went up and casually commenting that the paintings were "beautiful" and "ohhh, this one's really pretty, red is my favorite color." But this was more than "beautiful," more than "pretty" and not about my favorite color at all. How easy it is for us to complain about points in our lives that shape us. Whatever it is that they mean to us, we make them mean that. We can choose to grow from them. We can choose to accept that there, surrounding these rough edges are clouds and good times and love and flowers and sex and children and people and family and more real life.

I choose to live my life powerfully from this moment on. And on. And on.

Friday morning I was on my way out to a meeting. I was rushing out of the door when the phone rang. It was my Godmother (I call her my Godmother) V Kali calling from Los Angeles. There are certain folks who call who I just have to answer the phone for no matter how much I am rushing. V is one of those people. Normally our conversations go on and on but that morning she was all talked out before our conversation had even begun.

"Jaha, Zuri is dead." Those were her words. They came out of her mouth I am sure because they are still ringing in my ears right now. "Jaha, Zuri is dead." Period. No explanation mark. No screams. Just. Those. Words. I could hear the exhaustion in her voice. I could hear the story behind the syllabals. I could hear V being mommy.

Zuri is V's daughter. Twenty-nine. Just twenty-eight. Beautiful. Courageous. Bold. Sassy. Mother of three babies. She was going into a liquor store in Los Angeles and had left her son Omar in the car while she ran in real quick. *We do that. We kiss our babies, tell them we will be right back, and run in. Quick. And we are supposed to be right back. We are! We are! We are! She told him she would be right back and she should be with him now! She should because I just cannot sit with this!* As she was going in, or coming out, (I still don't know) she was caught up in a drive-by shooting and was shot in the stomach. *Even typing this right now is just too much to do. These are just words. These are words. What good are they? But people should know.* Of course she was not the intended victim. Of course. But she was there, right there coming out or going into the store. For what? How old school and played out are drive-by shootings?! How dangerous guns are in the hands of young men any day, but most especially I believe when Mercury is in retrograde. What does it mean? Please let it mean something. Please.

Years ago I asked V why artist go through the struggles we go through and what she said to me stuck. "Because we will tell it. And people need to know." And she said it again Friday morning. "Poets are here to bear witness and tell the stories." But not these stories.

Not this one.

But Life does not always hear my protests. Life does not usually. Life just goes on.

Jaha's greatest gift is that she can give yourself back to you. All those little pieces you've been holding back for fear of not being understood, the ones you pimped and the ones you ho'ed, the ones you loaned out and didn't get back and the ones that were straight up stolen. Jaha will give them back to you until you are the only you that you truly recognize and honor. That is the gift to inspire, the one that makes us all better even if sometimes it is only momentary.

You cannot pay Jaha what it cost her to live, experience, process and then turn into art this life she is inhabiting and you cannot pay for what it will mean to you as you read it and hear her voice come to life.

E. Amato